Usborne Naturetrail

Wild Flowers

Usborne Naturetrail
Wild Flowers

Sarah Khan and Kirsteen Rogers

Designed by
Michael Hill, Kate Rimmer,
Marc Maynard and Nayera Everall

Consultant: Dr Mark A. Spencer

Edited by Jane Chisholm

Internet links

There are lots of websites with information and activities for nature lovers. At the Usborne Quicklinks Website we have provided links to some great sites where you can:

- play a game to grow your own flower online
- watch time-lapse movies of seeds growing and flowers opening
- discover the secret lives of flowers
- take an animated tour through the life cycle of a plant
- explore online flower identification guides
- find out which flowers grow near your home
- dissect a virtual flower

For links to these sites, go to the Usborne Quicklinks Website at www.usborne-quicklinks.com and enter the keywords "naturetrail wild flowers".

CONTENTS

Looking at flowers

Making new flowers

Life and after

Wild flower habitats

60 Wild flowers to spot

Here are some of the places where wild flowers grow.

Rosebay willowherb grows at the side of railways.

White campion can be found in hedgerows.

Look for brooklime in marshes and by rivers.

Here are some of the many wild flowers you might spot growing on waste ground or in a country meadow.

Flowers in the wild

With their flimsy petals and delicate stalks, wild flowers like poppies and daisies may seem rather fragile. As a group of plants, though, they are really very tough. There have been flowering plants on Earth for over 145 million years, which makes flowers some of the best survivors on the planet. They can grow almost anywhere: from the hottest deserts to the coldest mountains and the dirtiest cities.

Originally, all flowers were wild; they just grew wherever they could. But, over time, people began to realize how useful flowers were, so they started growing them on purpose – for their looks, smell, taste, and to use as medicines. All the flowers people grow today have wild ancestors.

Field scabious

Hawkbit

Wild carrot

Looking for wild flowers

You're likely to see the widest variety of wild flowers in grassy, natural areas, but once you start looking, you may be surprised where they spring up. Most flowers need certain conditions to grow well. A plant's home, or habitat, provides all the things it needs to survive. Some flowers can grow almost anywhere. Others are fussier, so you'll only find them in certain places.

Yellow archangel is common in woods.

Sand dunes and cliffs are the best places to look for stonecrop.

Watercress usually grows in fast-flowing, chalky streams.

Shepherd's purse will grow pretty much anywhere.

Clumps of sea kale grow on pebbly beaches.

In the wild, flowers live and die at their own pace, and make seeds so new flowers can grow. If you pick them, though, there'll be fewer seeds, then fewer flowers – and some may disappear altogether. So look, but don't pick, and there'll always be wild flowers for everyone to enjoy.

Common butterwort can be found on mountains.

Greater knapweed

How a flower grows

A flower goes through several very different stages during its life. You might see young undeveloped flowers, curled up inside a bud, or others which have stopped flowering and turned into fruits and seeds.

Here you can see the life story of a poppy. All flowers (well, almost all) develop in a similar way.

Bud

1. A poppy plant grows from a seed. Buds form, with flowers curled up inside.

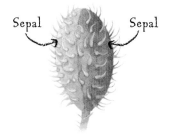

Sepal   Sepal

2. Leaf-like sepals protect the delicate petals. They begin to open as the flower grows.

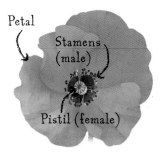

Petal   Stamens (male)

Pistil (female)

3. Inside the petals are male and female parts called the stamens and pistil.

Stigma

Ovary

4. The pistil is made of two parts: a sticky stigma on top and an ovary beneath.

Anther

5. Pod-like anthers on the tips of the stamens make a powder, called pollen.

6. A bee visits the poppy to feed. Pollen sticks to the bee, who takes it to another poppy.

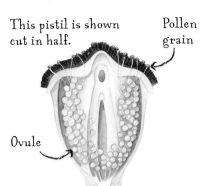

This pistil is shown cut in half.

Pollen grain

Ovule

7. The pollen rubs off onto a poppy's stigma. Tubes grow from the pollen down to egg-like ovules inside the ovary.

8. Pollen has tiny bits inside, which travel down the tubes into the ovules. The stamens and petals wilt and drop off.

9. Inside the pistil, the ovules start turning into seeds. The pistil swells, and is now called a fruit.

Hole

Seeds

10. The fruit ripens and its wall dries up. When the wind blows, the seeds are shaken out of holes, like pepper from a pot.

To make seeds, these poppies must have pollen from other poppies. Pollen from any other flowers just won't do.

Most wild flowers have the same basic bits and pieces, but they can look very different from each other.

Rosebay willowherb

Flower

Leaf

Stem

Roots

How plants live

Flowers are a plant's seed factories, making seeds that will grow into new plants. Other parts do different jobs to keep the plant alive.

During the day, leaves make food, using water, and a gas called carbon dioxide from the air. To do this, they need energy, which they absorb from sunlight. The stem is a plant's transport system. It has bundles of tubes inside that carry food and water to every part. Hidden underground, roots are busy too, taking water and goodness from the soil and fixing the plant to the spot.

Buds have undeveloped flowers or leaves inside. Flower buds are protected by leaf-like sepals.

The stem carries water from the roots to the leaves, and carries food from the leaves to the rest of the plant.

As well as making food, leaves take in gases from the air and release gases and water that the plant doesn't need.

The mesh of roots anchors the plant in the ground, stopping it from being blown or washed away.

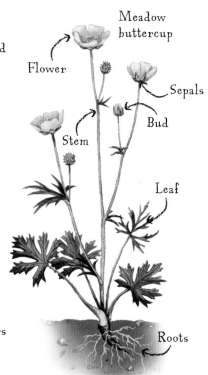

Meadow buttercup

Flower

Sepals

Bud

Stem

Leaf

Roots

Flower identification guides

You probably know the names of more wild flowers than you think. Try writing down all the ones you know, and see how many you get. To discover the names of flowers you don't know, you'll need a flower identification guide. This is a handy book filled with pictures of all kinds of different flowers, with tips on finding and identifying them. Here's the sort of information you'll find in a typical guide.

Many flower guides show a full-length picture of the flowering plant, and a close-up of its flower, too.

COMMON POPPY

Species: *Papaver rhoeas*
Family: *Papaveraceae*
In flower: Summer
Habitat: Fields and meadows

Each flower has a scientific name in Latin. This might not be the name you know it by.

This is where the flower usually grows in the wild.

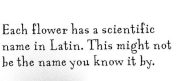

Seed pods develop in late summer.

Buds covered in small spikes

Height: up to 60cm (24in)

HANDY HINTS

To help you choose a flower guide, look up a flower you already know:
• Is it easy to find?
• Does the picture look like the flower?
• Are the words easy to read?
• Does it tell you what you want to know?

There are lots of flower identification guides to choose from. You can find a short one at the back of this book, starting on page 60, to help you begin spotting wild flowers straight away.

How to identify flowers

There are thousands and thousands of different wild flowers. That may seem a bit daunting, but if you look for the most obvious features, you'll soon learn to recognize the most common ones. The more you notice about a plant, the easier it'll be to look up. In your guide, the colour, size and shape of petals and sepals hold the biggest clues.

FLOWER ARRANGEMENTS

Look at the way flowers are arranged on a plant. Does each flower grow on a stem of its own? Or are there lots of small ones bunched together?

Each cornflower stem has a single flower head.

Each early purple orchid stem has several flowers growing around it.

Meadowsweet has clusters of small flowers.

The petals of this Lady's bedstraw make a cross shape.

Harebells are named after their bell-shaped flowers.

The hood is called a standard.

The lip is called a keel.

The petals of rest harrow flowers form a hood and lips.

Wood anemones are shaped like stars.

Greater bindweed flowers are trumpet shaped.

Spur

Larkspur flowers form a tube called a spur.

Looking at leaves

Leaves can help you identify a plant, too. Do they have one overall shape or does each stalk have several leafy parts, known as leaflets? Do these look hairy or bumpy, smooth or spiky? Colours range from dull grey, red and purple, to bronze, silver and gold, as well as almost every imaginable shade of green.

Lesser celandine has heart-shaped leaves.

The leaves of brooklime are oval with toothed edges.

Lobe

White bryony has lobed leaves.

Common centaury leaves are smooth and narrow.

Sea holly has prickly silvery blue-green leaves.

Each Alpine milk vetch leaf is made up of smaller leaflets.

LEAF ARRANGEMENTS

Here are a few of the different ways that leaves can be arranged on a stem.

Sand spurrey leaves grow along the stems in opposite pairs.

Leaves of white helleborine sit alternately along the stem.

Ice plant leaves grow in spirals up the stem.

Rosettes of primrose leaves grow around the base of the stem.

Wild flower calendar

Most flowers bloom in spring and summer, but some wait until autumn before opening their petals. A few even thrive in the icy frost and snow of winter. This calendar shows you just a few of the flowers you might see if you go out spotting in different seasons.

Winter

Snowdrop

Winter aconite

Butterbur

Daisy

Spring

Wild daffodil

Greater stitchwort

Primrose

Bird's-foot trefoil

Wood anemone

Common dog violet

Cowslip

Sweet violet

Summer

Snapdragon

Purple loosestrife

Red campion

Enchanter's nightshade

Meadowsweet

Sweet William

Blackberry

Musk mallow

Larkspur

Dog rose

Bats-in-the-belfry

Yellow pimpernel

Autumn

Soapwort

Field scabious

Autumn crocus

Autumn feltwort

Keeping a flower diary

You could try keeping a record of flowers you've seen. Start by making rough notes and sketches of flowers when you're out and about. At the end of a trip, you could copy them into a flower diary, noting when and where you saw the flowers. You could include drawings, photos and leaf rubbings, too. As you add to your diary over the year, you'll also build up a picture of how plants change with the seasons.

You could decorate your diary with pressed flowers.

SPOTTING TIP

Useful things to take on a flower spotting trip:
• Notepad (spiral bound ones are best)
• Pencils
• Tape measure
• Camera
• Magnifying glass

July 12th

Stour Meadows
Warm and sunny

Golden flowers, flat on top

Flowers are 20mm across.

Flowers look like daisies.

Hairy stem

Spear-shaped leaves

Plant is 40cm high.

Wavy edges

Common fleabane

16

Pressing flowers

You can press flowers to stick in your diary or to decorate cards, notepaper, bookmarks and gift tags. Only use garden or bought flowers, though, not ones growing in the wild.

1. Pick some clean, dry, fully opened flowers. Choose flowers that are naturally flat, such as violas, petunias and primulas.

2. Lay a piece of blotting paper on one page of an old book. Put the flowers on the paper and lay another piece of paper over them.

3. Close the book and stack more books on top. Leave the flowers there for at least two weeks until they're dry and flat.

Rubbing leaves

Rubbing leaves makes prints of their shapes and the pattern on their surface. You could make leaf rubbings in your notebook or, like pressed flowers, use them to decorate things.

Your rubbing will show up the patterns on the leaf.

1. Find a clean, dry, flat leaf and put it on a piece of paper.

2. Place more paper on top. Rub gently over it with a crayon or pencil.

You could arrange a few leaves in a group before rubbing them.

Growing wild flowers

These wild flowers are easy to grow.

Knapweed

Bugle

Flower

Field scabious

One of the best ways to watch wild flowers change is to grow some of your own from seeds. You can buy these from garden centres and nurseries. Some packets contain mixed wild flower seeds; others have just one kind. If you're growing plants that usually flower in summer, start growing the seeds indoors, in early spring. Then, when they've grown into baby plants (seedlings, in plant-speak), you can move them outside, once the weather's warm.

Cornflowers like these are becoming rare in the wild, but you can grow your own from a packet of seeds.

How to grow wild flowers

To grow some wild flowers, you will need: a seed tray with holes in the bottom; compost; wild flower seeds; trowel; dibber or stick; watering can; plastic food wrap; several 7cm (3in) pots; three or more 15cm (6in) pots.

Push the seeds with your finger.

1. Fill the tray with compost to 2cm (1in) below the rim. Sow the seeds following the instructions on the packet.

2. Scatter compost on top. Stretch food wrap over the tray. Keep it in a light place until green shoots appear.

Check how damp the compost is every day.

3. Take off the food wrap as soon as shoots grow. Water the tray if the compost feels dry when you press the top.

Pick the seedlings that look most healthy.

4. Half fill the small pots with compost. Push the dibber or stick into the soil by a seedling and lift up its roots and soil.

Hold onto the lower leaves as you lift.

5. Hold the seedling in a pot. Fill in around it with compost. Do the same for each seedling. Keep the pots inside.

6. After a few weeks, if the weather is warm, partly fill the bigger pots with compost, as shown here.

Tap the bottom of the pot.

7. Put a finger on either side of the stem of the healthiest-looking plant. Turn its pot over and tip the seedling and compost out.

8. Hold the plant by its stem and put it in a big pot. Fill compost around it. Do the same for a few more plants. Place the pots outside.

These flowers are especially attractive to butterflies.

Candytuft

Michaelmas daisy

Willow gentian

This flat, orange flower makes a handy landing pad for lots of insects, including butterflies.

Showing off

Many flowers make a sweet, syrupy liquid called nectar to attract insects. Some insects eat pollen, too. The shape and colour of their petals often advertises these tasty treats, just as attractive shop window displays tempt customers inside. In spring and summer, look for insects feeding on flowers, and see if you can spot which ones go where.

Insects keep a look out for flowers that will be convenient for them to feed from. Those with short mouthparts, such as bees and flies, tend to prefer flowers with a shallow saucer, star, or cross shape. But flowers shaped like trumpets, funnels or long cups are better suited to moths and butterflies. This is because they have long, curly tongues that can reach down to the nectar at the bottom of the petals.

Seeing signals

Insects see colours differently from people, and are drawn to colours that stand out the most to them. For example, bees are often attracted to yellow and blue flowers, while butterflies tend to flit towards pinks, reds and oranges. Moths – which fly around at night – visit white and cream flowers, because they're easier to see in the dark.

To a person, an evening primrose looks plain creamy-yellow...

...but, to a bee, it looks blue with vivid stripes and patches in the middle.

The dots on these foxgloves guide bees as they crawl inside to get to the nectar.

The reason bees see things differently is because they can sense ultraviolet light, a type of light that's invisible to people. This enables them to see marks that other creatures can't. These marks form patterns that lead them to the heart of the flower, where nectar is made – a bit like airport runway lights showing pilots where to land.

Some petals have nectar guides that you can see, too. How many different examples of stripes, splodges and spots can you find?

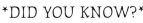

DID YOU KNOW?

In some countries, birds, bats, mice, and even monkeys drink nectar and eat pollen from wild flowers.

A snapdragon's smell is made up of just seven different oils...

...while an orchid has 100 oils to make its scent.

Making scents

When you're out and about spotting flowers, you'll notice that many of them have a nice smell. This comes from oils in their petals, sepals, pollen or nectar. For thousands of years, people have used flower petals to scent their homes, and have made them into perfumes to make themselves smell sweet, too.

But flowers don't just smell good to please people. Their scented oils are a signal to insects, usually to let them know that they have a tasty supply of pollen and nectar to feed on. Each type of flower has a different combination of oils to make its own, distinctive smell – anything from seven to as many as a hundred different oils.

Lavender has a strong, sweet scent that attracts bees and butterflies.

Day scents

Not all perfumed flowers smell 24 hours a day. Some turn off their scents at night by folding up their petals to protect their insides from the cold, and early morning dew. Insects can't feed when the flowers are closed, so the flowers don't release their oils then. But, in the morning, they unfold their petals and let their fragrance waft out, telling insects that they're open for business again.

These flowers are scented only during the day.

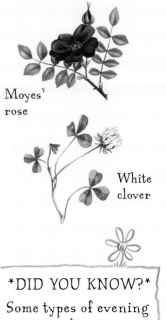

Moyes' rose

White clover

A Pasque flower closes at night.

In the morning, it opens up again to tempt insects with its scent and colour.

DID YOU KNOW?

Some types of evening primrose burst open so quickly at night that they make a popping sound.

Night scents

Some flowers are open all the time, but don't smell very strongly until night falls. Then, they release heavily-scented oils to attract moths and other night insects. Other flowers wait until night before they open at all. Night-scented flowers usually smell more strongly than day-scented ones, to help insects find them in the dark.

Peach blossom moth

Honeysuckle is especially strongly scented at night.

Hover fly

Drone fly

Large wing

Small wing

Honey bee, with two pairs of wings

Pollen-movers

The reason why flowers do so much to attract insects – using their shape, colour and smell – is because they need the insects to move their pollen to another flower of the same kind. This is the only way for most flowers to make seeds, which will grow into new plants. Many types of plant would die out completely if insects didn't do this vital job for them.

Insects don't move pollen on purpose, though – it happens by accident as they fly from flower to flower in search of food.

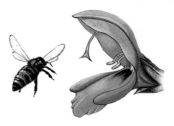

1. As a bee drinks from a meadow clary flower, its body gets covered in pollen.

2. The bee flies to another flower, carrying the first flower's pollen on its body.

3. The pollen brushes off the bee's body, onto the flower's stigma.

4. As the bee takes another drink, it gets dusted with new pollen, and off it goes again...

The pale specks you can see on this bee's hairy body are grains of lavender pollen.

Sticking on

It can be a risky journey for a grain of hitchhiking pollen. It has to avoid being blown away as its pilot flies through the air, or being brushed off as its chauffeur creeps along the ground. Some pollen is sticky or spiky, so it can fix itself onto an insect. Some flowers, such as many orchids, go one step further by packing their pollen into waxy bags that clip onto insects' heads as they feed.

Tiny yellow powder-filled packages of orchid pollen stick to bee's heads.

DID YOU KNOW?

Slugs and snails are slow but steady pollen-movers. As they slither and slide from one flower to another, they ooze thick slime, which pollen sticks to.

Most insects that feed from flowers, such as bees, wasps and butterflies, have tiny hairs on their bodies. The bees brush past the stamens as they push into the flowers to reach the nectar, and the sticky pollen clings to their hairs.

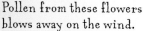

Pollen from these flowers blows away on the wind.

Pigweed pollen

Nettle pollen

Broad-leaved dock pollen

Pollen in the air

Not all flowers need insects to carry pollen for them – some let their pollen blow away on the wind. Just as spiky or sticky pollen is well-designed for latching onto passing insects, so wind-spread pollen is ideally shaped for catching the lightest breeze. Ragweeds, for instance, have grains of round, dimpled pollen that soar through the air like mini golf balls.

The pollen of most grasses and trees is spread in this way. It's this airborne pollen that gives some people hayfever in the spring and summer, making them sniff and sneeze.

The yellow blobs on these hare's tail flowers are stamens covered in pollen.

Catching the wind

To flowers whose pollen is spread by air, being brightly coloured or deliciously scented isn't important. Their aim is to catch the wind – not to attract visitors – so their small, light pollen needs to be easily accessible.

You can often tell which flowers use the wind to spread pollen because their stamens are literally hanging around, waiting for a breeze. The further they dangle, the better, so each gust can catch as much pollen as possible.

Ribwort plantain

Hoary plantain

Greater plantain

These flowers have stamens that hang out, exposed to any passing breath of air.

Doing it for themselves

To grow seeds, most flowers need pollen from another flower of the same type. But a few can manage perfectly well without – they can use their own. When pollen drops from their stamens onto their stigmas, seeds start to grow. If their pollen hasn't dropped (or been carried away by visitors), some flowers can even move it themselves.

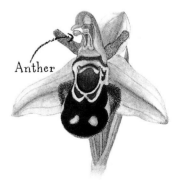

Anther

A bee orchid moves pollen by bending its anthers down towards its stigma, which is inside the lower petal.

Protecting pollen

Grains of pollen are fragile and can easily be
washed away by rain or dew, or damaged by
extreme temperatures. It's a flower's job to
protect its precious pollen from these dangers.

Sheltering shapes

A flower's shape affects how much protection
it can offer. When it's raining, you might see
raindrops trickling down the petals of bell- or
umbrella-shaped flowers. These drooping
flowers make a good shelter for pollen, as
water can't collect inside them.

The upper petal of this
broom flower keeps the
rain off its pollen.

Some flowers have petals that
act like umbrellas – the rain
rolls right off them.

Snowdrops

Bluebells

When a bee lands on the
lower petal, it bends,
exposing the stamens.

The petals of some flowers, such as broom
and snapdragons, form hinged pouches. Most
of the time they're firmly closed, with their
powdery treasure safe inside. When an insect
lands, they open up – but only if it's big and
heavy enough to prise open the flowery jaws.

Moving petals

Some flowers protect their pollen by only opening their petals when the weather is warm and sunny. If the temperature drops, the petals close and the pollen stays safe.

Many flowers have regular opening and closing times, spreading their petals after dawn and folding them away again at dusk. This protects their pollen from the lowest temperatures and from the damp droplets of morning dew and evening mist.

Some Pasque flowers bend their stalks in the rain, so the flowers hang down like bells rather than sitting upright like cups.

Morning glory gets its name from its habit of opening during the day.

Daisies open their petals in the day and close them at night.

Open flowers

Closed flowers

TRY THIS

Flowers can tell if it's dark or light. To see this for yourself, put two house plants of the same type, both with open flowers, on a sunny windowsill. Cover one with a box to block out the light. Leave them for a few hours, then lift up the box. What do you see?

Flower   Fruit

Sorrel fruits can be
carried away on the wind.

Flower   Fruit

Red campion seeds grow
in pods and are shaken
out by the wind.

Flower   Fruit

Dandelion fruits have
white, silky "parachutes"
that catch the wind.

Flower   Fruit

A sea rocket seed pod drops
into the water, and opens
to let its seeds float away.

Fruits and seeds

Once flowers' stigmas have the pollen they need,
new life begins. The ovaries turn into fruits and,
hidden inside them, tiny ovules slowly ripen
into seeds. When a seed is ripe and ready, it
needs to find a place of its own, with enough
space and light for it to grow into a flower.
If a fruit just falls to the ground, the seed will
be in the shadow of its parent, and won't
be able to grow properly. So the further
away it can move, the better.

Floating and sailing

Looking closely at seeds or fruits can sometimes
give you a clue as to how they might have
travelled. Some have hairs or wings, that help
them catch the wind. Some don't need flying
equipment at all – they're so small and light
that the slightest breeze can carry them away.

For fruits that grow in or near water,
spreading seeds can be as easy as letting them
drop down and sail away. The seeds are often
light enough to float, and have a coating to
protect them from water damage. Sometimes
the whole fruit drops into the water before
opening up to release its seeds.

Popping out

Some seeds explode into the world. Either their fruits burst open, or the threads that attach them to the fruit suddenly snap, and they shoot into the air.

A herb Robert seed pod opens with a sudden spring action and flings its seeds into the air.

Hitching a ride

If you see a seed or fruit that's covered in tiny hooks, it's probably a hitchhiker. The hooks catch onto the fur of passing animals, or cling to people's clothes as they brush past. The seed is carried away and eventually falls off.

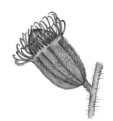

Agrimony fruits have hooks that latch onto fur or clothing.

Animals also help spread seeds by eating them. As they munch on fruit, they either drop the seeds onto the ground or swallow them. Swallowed seeds pass through animals undamaged and come out in their droppings.

By eating these blackberries, this squirrel is helping spread seeds.

These wild flowers
grow from bulbs.

Winter aconite

Lesser celandine

Wild daffodil

New plants from old

When it comes to making new plants, many
wild flowers don't leave anything to chance.
After a chilly summer, with fewer insects,
their whole future could be in peril. So, as
well as making pollen, flowers often have
other cunning ways of producing offspring.

Underground larders

As winter approaches, some old, dying plants
form a food store called a bulb or a corm. A bulb
is a type of scaly underground stem, like a tiny
onion. It contains food, layers of leaves and the
beginnings of a new stem and roots.

Corms are similar, but without the layers.
When its time's up, the plant above the ground
dies away. But, hidden below, the store stays alive
and, in the next year, a fresh, new plant emerges.

Each of these spring
crocuses has grown
from a corm below
the ground.

Honeysuckle makes seeds but can also grow from stems called runners.

Keep on running

Some plants grow long side stems called runners. When a runner touches the ground, it develops roots of its own and starts to grow into a new plant. At first, the parent plant sends food through the runner to its offspring. But, once it can live on its own, the runner rots away and the new plant is left to fend for itself.

Silverweed develops red, hairy runners.

Strawberry plant

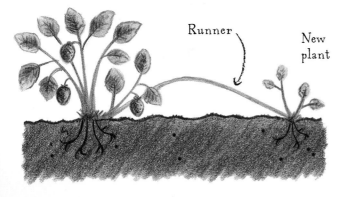

Runner

New plant

Soapwort can grow from seeds or rhizomes.

Rhizomes are thick underground runners that grow out sideways from a plant's roots. New roots sprout from the bottom of a rhizome, and shoots grow from knobbly buds on top. Roots and buds can grow at any point along it. So, with the help of one rhizome, a plant can quickly and stealthily take over a wide area. Mint and most grasses spread this way.

Greater bindweed spreads rapidly however it can – by seeds, runners or rhizomes.

33

Look out for these plants
that live less than a year.

Love lies
bleeding

Corn cockle

Red campion

Ivy-
leaved
toadflax

How long do flowers live?

Even the toughest plants can't live for ever
and each plant has its own natural lifespan,
which is the time it takes to grow, flower,
develop fruit and spread seeds. Some plants
do these things once in their lives; others
repeat them year after year. Once a plant
has come to the end of its lifespan, it dies.

One year...

Plants that only last a single year are called
annuals. Some go from a seed to a dead plant
in just a few months. Annuals usually grow
and flower during the spring, develop fruit in
the summer and die by the end of autumn.
Their seeds lie resting over winter, ready to
grow into new flowers the following spring.

...or two?

Biennial plants last for two years. In their first
year, they grow and store food. In the second,
they flower, make seeds and die.
Their seeds grow into new
flowers the following year.

Viper's bugloss spends one year
growing and storing food. The
next year it flowers, makes and
spreads seeds, then dies.

Long-lasting plants

Some plants can live for years, growing and flowering every spring. These are called perennials. In winter, some or all of the parts that are above the ground wither away, but the roots remain alive, using up food stored in them over spring and summer. When spring comes again, a new flower grows from these roots.

These plants can live for many years.

Bloody crane's-bill

Anemone

Unexpected flowers

The most unpredictable kinds of plant are called ephemerals. You may not see anything of an ephemeral plant for months, or even years. Then, as soon as the plant has the growing conditions it needs, it will quickly grow, flower, develop seeds and die. Depending on the plant, this whole cycle can be over in less than a month.

Chickweed seeds can lie resting in an unused field for years and years, but spring to life when the field is ploughed.

Secrets of survival

A plant's life is not an easy one. If it manages to survive the heat and cold, flood and drought, it still has to escape creatures that want to eat it. Plants may not be able to run, but many still have ways to dodge predators, call for help, hide and even fight back. What's more amazing is that you usually won't be able to tell when it's happening: most plants do all this without moving a millimetre.

Stinging and scratching

If you look closely, you'll see that some plants have stiff spines, sharp thorns, pointy prickles or stinging hairs growing on them. These are there to put animals off eating them – the plant's way of saying, "Leave me alone!" It tells them that chewing and swallowing it would be painful.

WARNING
If you don't want to risk getting pricked or stung, avoid touching plants with thorns, prickles, spines or hairs.

Rough poppy stems are hairy and their sepals are covered in bristles.

Blackberry stems are thorny.

Common teasels are covered in sturdy spines.

Scents and poisons

Some plants can call for help by releasing scents into the air. When cabbage white caterpillars take their first nibble of a wild cabbage leaf, the plant lets rip with an unusual smell. This is picked up by braconid wasps, which eat cabbage white caterpillars. They know that if they follow the scent, they'll soon find a juicy snack.

Wild cabbage flowers can make a special smell to call for help in emergencies.

   Many plants defend themselves by making poisonous chemicals in their leaves when they're being eaten. Some give off these poisons in their scent too, so any passing animals know to leave them alone.

These flowers are all poisonous.

Black nightshade   Yellow iris   Ragwort

Buttercup   Pellitory-of-the-wall   Autumn crocus

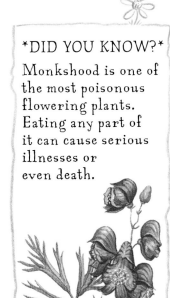

DID YOU KNOW?
Monkshood is one of the most poisonous flowering plants. Eating any part of it can cause serious illnesses or even death.

Sweet violet flowers are used to flavour desserts.

Rape seeds are squeezed to get cooking oil out of them.

Broom flowers make a yellow dye.

Using flowers

Flowers come in such a range of colours and shapes that people all over the world use them as decorations in their homes and gardens, and as symbols in celebrations and religious ceremonies. But flowers aren't just pretty to look at – for centuries, people have been discovering plenty of practical uses for them, too.

Cooking and colouring

Have you ever eaten a flower? Using flowers in cooking isn't as unusual as you might think. Parts of flowering plants, such as petals, leaves and roots are used to flavour food. Some petals can even be eaten raw and rose petals give Turkish delight its colour and taste. Lots of flowers, including jasmine, rose, chamomile, cowslip and comfrey, are used to make tea.

Cowslip

Boiling flowers is also a good way to make dyes. Lots of flowers, such as barberry, broom and ragwort, will colour the water they are boiled in. That water can then be used to dye fabric or even hair. It's not just petals that make dyes; brilliant colours can be extracted from roots, berries and leaves, too.

Medicines

Throughout history, plants have been used as medicines, to treat everything from colds to cholera. Today, people still use natural remedies, such as tea made from ginger to cure a sore throat or an upset stomach. Scientists use plants as ingredients in modern medicines, too. Foxgloves, for example, are used to make digoxin, a drug to treat heart disease.

Lavender and chamomile lotions can be used to treat burns, boils and insect bites.

Flowery fragrances

Scents from sweet-smelling flowers can be extracted to make perfume. This is done by boiling the flowers, cooling the steam and collecting droplets of scented oil from it. Thousands of petals are needed to make a tiny amount of the oil, so perfumes made with pure flower oil are very expensive. Most perfume-makers use chemicals instead.

The scented oils of lily-of-the-valley are extracted and used to make sweet, light perfumes.

DID YOU KNOW?

People have been making perfume for thousands of years. To make themselves smell nice, Ancient Egyptians soaked petals in fat, and moulded it into cones to put on their heads.

Look out for these flowers
in walls and pavements.

Yarrow

Purslane

Houseleek

Towns and cities

Towns might not seem the most promising places to start a wild flower search, but if you keep your eyes peeled, you'll see them all around. Look in streets and car parks, waste ground and building sites, parks, gardens and churchyards. You'll often find flowers growing in unlikely places: in between paving stones, in walls, even in cracks in buildings – anywhere where they can find enough soil.

Most of these flowers are weeds – plants that grow where they're not wanted – and their seeds are usually spread by the wind.

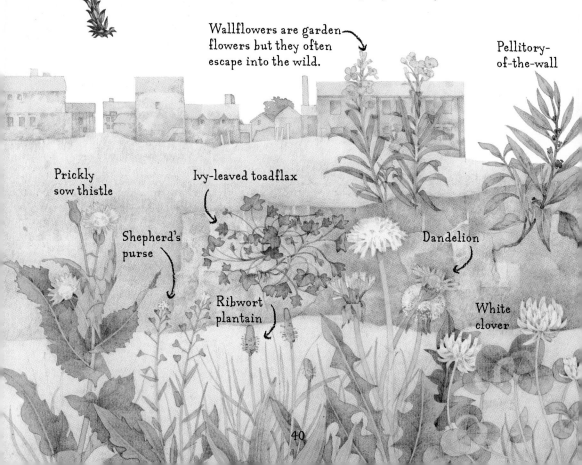

Wallflowers are garden flowers but they often escape into the wild.

Pellitory-of-the-wall

Prickly sow thistle

Ivy-leaved toadflax

Shepherd's purse

Dandelion

Ribwort plantain

White clover

40

Weeds

Some weeds behave like vandals, tearing up road surfaces and widening cracks in pipes and walls. They're a quick-spreading menace in gardens, using water and light needed by plants that gardeners work so hard to grow. Others do no harm, though, and some can even be useful, providing birds and insects with food and a safe place to lay their eggs.

DID YOU KNOW?

Oxford ragwort grows well in building sites and by railways, where it's dusty and dry. It originally grew on the parched, ashy sides of Mount Etna, a volcano in Italy.

Common toadflax

Evening primrose

Wall pennywort

Oxford ragwort

Rosebay willowherb

Scented mayweed

White campion

Daisy

Hedgerows

When you set off into the country in search of wild flowers, probably the first things you'll come across are hedgerows. These bushes and banks shelter the sides of roads and fields and provide a safe home for all sorts of wild flowers.

Dog rose

Wild clematis

High branches screen them from cold and stormy weather, blocking gusty winds, and catching flurries of snow in winter. Fallen autumn leaves blanket the ground underneath, protecting flowers from frost. As they rot, they release nutrients into the soil too, making it rich and nourishing.

Cow parsley

Honeysuckle

Hedgerows are full of life, providing food and shelter for different kinds of wild flowers, birds and animals.

Common teasel

Stinging nettle

Foxglove

Survival challenge

With all these benefits, it's hardly surprising that hedgerows are so popular. In fact, overcrowding is often a problem and each plant has to struggle for space to grow.

The tall hedges that make such efficient windbreaks can also block out the sun and rain. In their shadow, competition for sunlight and water can be fierce. Many flowers survive by climbing – clinging to branches for support as they scramble up towards the light. Meanwhile, in the soil below, the battle for water is fought unseen, as tangled roots stretch and strain to soak up every last drop.

Even visits from animals that will move pollen or spread seeds can't be taken for granted. Flowers fill the hedgerows with bright, richly scented displays of petals or fruits as they vie for their attention.

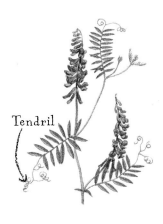

Dog roses use their sharp thorns to grip onto other plants, as they climb up to reach the light.

Tendril

Tufted vetch winds its curly tendrils around hedge branches.

Flowers growing on grassy verges at the roadside have to survive car exhaust fumes.

Herb Robert

Greater stitchwort

Creeping cinquefoil

Wild strawberry

These flowers are common in fields and meadows.

Oxeye daisy

Hogweed

Bird's-foot trefoil

Creeping buttercup

Fields and meadows

Nothing may seem more natural than grassy pastures full of wild flowers. But it's the fact that they're regularly mown, by machines or the chomping teeth of hungry animals, that allows such a wide variety to survive. If they weren't cut back, the stronger species would rampage across the fields, and smother the weaker flowers out of existence.

Wild flowers spring up in crops, too. Farmers sometimes regard them as weeds, because they take valuable space, water and food away from crops, or poison livestock. Some farmers get rid of them by digging them up or spraying them with chemicals. Flowers are also harmed indirectly by chemicals used to kill pests, which often kill pollen-movers, too.

Next time you're in a field or meadow, try counting how many kinds of wild flowers you can spot.

Meadow thistle

Common comfrey

Red clover

Protecting wildlife

Recently, many farmers have started setting aside strips at the edges of fields, or even whole fields, where wildlife can thrive. Some also use ways to control weeds and pests that don't do such widespread damage to other plant or insect communities. Here are three flowers to look out for in wild areas on farmland.

Cornflower

Corn spurrey

Snake's head fritillary

Meadowsweet

Yellow rattle

Common valerian

Wild pansy

Oak
leaves

Oak fruit
(acorns)
in autumn

Oak woods

In oak woods in spring, you may be lucky
enough to find spectacular carpets of flowers
such as primroses and bluebells. At this time
of year, growing conditions are good. The
soil is rich with decaying leaves, trees give
protection from the wind and, while the
branches are still bare, there's plenty of light.

In summer, it's a different story. The
woods are darker, as the leafy canopy shades
the woodland floor, so you'll find most
flowers in clearings or by paths. Some light
still filters through, though, and a few
flowers can thrive in the dappled light.

Spring and early summer
are the best times for
spotting flowers
in oak woods.

Look for these flowers growing
in oak woods in spring.

Primrose   Wood anemone   Lesser periwinkle   Wood sorrel

In summer, you might find these
flowers in an oak wood.

Foxglove   Red campion   Enchanter's nightshade   Wood woundwort

47

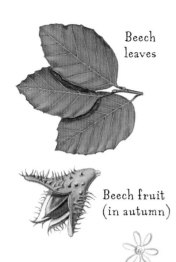

Beech leaves

Beech fruit (in autumn)

SPOTTING TIP

It's hard for flowers to grow in conifer woods, because the trees have leaves on them all year round. You're most likely to find flowers in summer, in areas where trees have been cut down.

Norway spruce tree

Beech woods

Flowers that grow in beech woods prefer thin soil that doesn't hold much water. Like oaks, beeches shed their leaves each autumn, but the leaves break down so slowly that a thick layer of leaf litter covers the ground all year. Plant seedlings struggle to push through these dead leaves to the light.

You'll find the most flowers in areas with the fewest trees, for example along paths and by streams. In spring, look out for carpets of bluebells in clearings or at the edges of the woods. In summer, the leaves form a dense canopy, which blocks the sunlight, casting deep shadows. Only a few flowers can grow in the dim light of a beechwood summer.

The leafy branches of these closely growing beech trees prevent much light from reaching the forest floor.

Here are some flowers you might
see in beech woods in spring.

Common dog violet   Arum   Sweet woodruff   Bluebell

These flowers grow in beech
woods during the summer.

Bats-in-the-belfry   Golden rod   Red helleborine   Wood avens

Little air pockets in duckweed plants enable them to float on the water's surface.

Flowers

Mare's tails can grow completely under water. They have tiny green flowers with no petals.

Ponds and streams

Plants can flourish in a range of watery habitats, from cool, green ponds to clear, tumbling streams or fast-flowing rivers. But water isn't the most stable of environments. Heavy rains might fill a pond to overflowing, and then a dry spell might shrink it to a puddle. Even a light breeze sends ripples racing over the surface. So plants have adapted in ingenious ways.

Some have roots that reach right down, anchoring them in the soft mud. Their long, flexible stems allow the flowers to float on the surface, whether the water rises or falls. Other plants just drift around, absorbing nutrients from the water through their trailing roots.

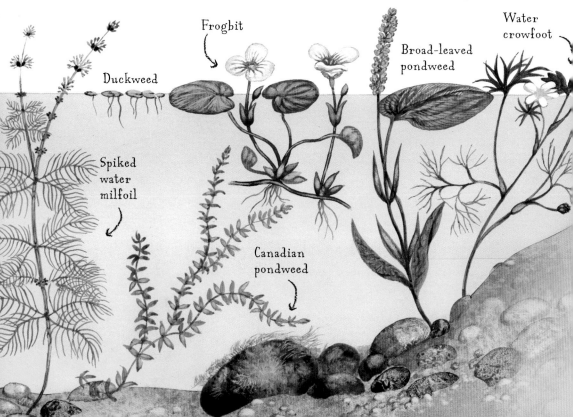

Duckweed

Frogbit

Broad-leaved pondweed

Water crowfoot

Spiked water milfoil

Canadian pondweed

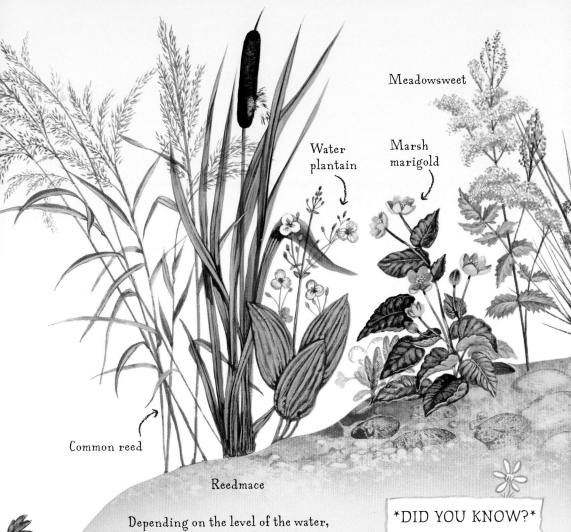

Meadowsweet

Water
plantain

Marsh
marigold

Common reed

Reedmace

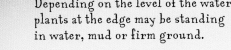

Depending on the level of the water,
plants at the edge may be standing
in water, mud or firm ground.

Pollen and seeds

Flowers above the water usually
have their pollen moved by insects
or the wind. Most that grow under
the surface release their pollen into
the water and it floats away. When
they develop into fruits, the seeds
are spread in the same way.

DID YOU KNOW?
Water lilies often
close and dip below
the surface at night.
When their fruits
are ripe, they sink
to the bottom of the
pond before releasing
up to 2,000 seeds.

Flexible
stem

By the seashore

Sunny weather, sea breezes and salty air make coasts popular spots for tourists, but, for the plants that live there, life's a constant battle for survival. Strong sea winds can easily uproot plants that are too tall or aren't anchored firmly enough to the ground.

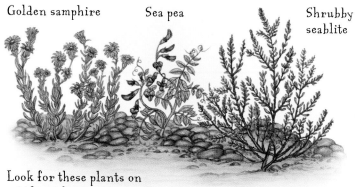

Golden samphire   Sea pea   Shrubby seablite

Look for these plants on pebbly or firm sandy beaches.

Some plants can be found on the beach itself. They have long, sprawling roots to hold them fast while the sand and pebbles shift with the tides. Roots also need to go deep for fresh water and nutrients.

Sea lyme grass   Sea couch grass   Marram grass   Sea rocket

Sea sandwort

Saving water

You might think plants near the sea have more than enough water, but they're actually always in danger of drying out. Sea water is too salty to use, and strong, salty breezes and bright sunshine can soon wither plants unless they find ways to protect the water inside them.

Sand dunes

The best spots for survival are where there's shelter from the wind, sea and sun. Low sandy hills, called dunes, can offer exactly this. Most flowers grow on the side facing away from the sea, often forming creeping mats on the ground, where they're less exposed to strong winds.

The leaves of these plants help them save water in different ways.

The hairy leaves of yellow horned poppies catch drops of dew and rain.

Sea holly leaves have a thick, waxy skin to keep the water in.

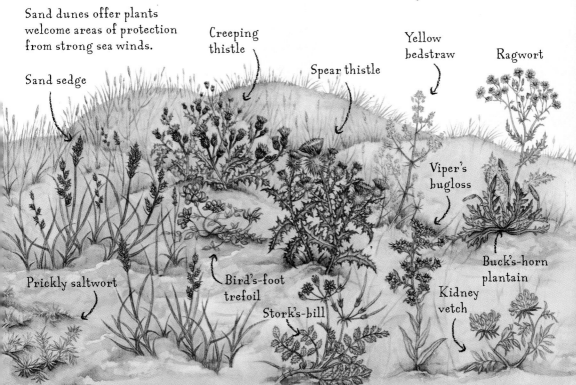

Sand dunes offer plants welcome areas of protection from strong sea winds.

Sand sedge

Creeping thistle

Spear thistle

Yellow bedstraw

Ragwort

Viper's bugloss

Sand sedge

Prickly saltwort

Bird's-foot trefoil

Stork's-bill

Kidney vetch

Buck's-horn plantain

Sea campion

Rock samphire

Wild cabbage

Thrift

Rock sea spurrey

Sea kale

Sea cliffs

From a distance, towering sea cliffs often look barren, which is hardly surprising, as conditions there are so hostile. Plants that dare to grow are constantly buffeted by gales and lashed with salty sea spray, which draws fresh water out of them. When it rains, it often pours. But even on the flat ledges and clifftops, the rainwater trickles quickly away between the rocks.

Flowers that thrive often have deep, wide-spreading roots, which hold them fast and reach into cracks and crevices where rainwater collects.

Without long roots to anchor them, these three tall, clifftop flowers would soon be blown away.

Golden rod

Red valerian

Wild cabbage

Many plants grow low, to keep out of the wind. A few sprout from nooks on perilous ledges, but you'll find most flowers peppering the wiry grass on clifftops, where there's more soil.

Here are some of the plants that grow on cliffs.

Salt marshes

Salt marshes are found in low-lying areas near the coast. Regular flooding by high tides turns the land into a boggy mixture of mud, sand and salt water. Some plants have developed specialized ways to survive in these salty surroundings.

Sea lavender, for example, stores excess salt in bumps on its leaves, which burst to release the salt. Annual seablite can store fresh water in its fleshy leaves.

Areas close to the sea are flooded twice a day. This is just too much salt and water for many plants, so you'll find more varieties growing on parts of the marshes that are further away from the sea.

Look for these flowers on the upper salt marshes, beyond the reach of the usual daily tides.

These salt-marsh plants can cope with frequent washings of salty water, so they grow near to the sea.

Annual
seablite

Sea arrow
grass

WARNING

Take care when you walk on salt marshes as it's easy to sink into the mud. Go with a friend and wear rubber boots.

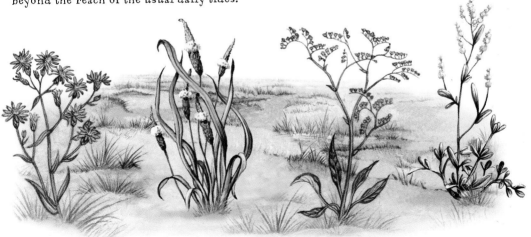

Sea aster   Sea plantain   Sea lavender   Sea purslane

Moors and heaths

Moors and heaths are wide open areas of land that are usually swept by wind. Some are very dry, but in others, frequent heavy rain clogs up the soil and washes nutrients away. You'll find fewer flowers on moors and heaths than in meadows and fields. But the ones that do grow, such as heather and gorse, sometimes take over large areas.

Here are some plants that can grow low to survive the windy conditions on heaths and moorland.

Here are some of the flowers you can find on moors and heaths.

Gorse

Sheep's bit

Bell heather

Gorse

Bell heather

Sundew

Sheep's bit

56

Marshes

Marshes are open, grassy areas that are waterlogged for some or all of the year – a bit like wet meadows. The ground is often so full of water that there isn't much air for the roots to breathe. Marsh plants often have tiny pockets of air inside their leaves and stems. This air can be pumped to the roots to stop them from drowning.

Many marsh plants, like these, have large leaves, so the plants can lose excess water through them.

These common flowers thrive in bogs and marshes.

Meadowsweet

Great willowherb

Common meadowrue

Ragged Robin

Water avens

Marsh marigold

Marsh violet

Harebell

Bilberry

In the mountains

How many types of mountain flowers can you spot here?

Freezing temperatures, cruel winds, dry ground and poor soil make mountains the ultimate endurance challenge. The higher up you go, the fewer flowers you'll find. A number of species have learned to survive, though, and in spring, brighten the bleak landscape with flowers.

Strong winds can uproot flowers, so they have to grow long roots over a wide area to grip the ground. Some roots even work their way into cracks in rocks for extra security. Many mountain flowers grow in low, thick mats, which leave less of the plant exposed to the howling wind.

Helpful leaves

All plants lose water through their leaves and many mountain plants have small leaves, to avoid losing too much. Some are hairy too, to keep them warm and catch water droplets.

These mountain flowers have all found ways to survive the harsh conditions.

Common butterwort

Alpine forget-me-not

Alpine milk vetch

Opposite-leaved golden saxifrage

Alpine Lady's mantle

Alpine rock cress

Starry saxifrage

Moss campion

Alpine fleabane

Wild flowers to spot

In this section of the book, you'll find pictures and descriptions of wild flowers to spot. They tell you where and when to look, as well as useful facts about their height or length and distinctive features. The flowers are grouped by colour.

You can find links to more flower identification guides on the Usborne Quicklinks Website at *www.usborne-quicklinks.com*

Flower

Harebell

10–25cm (4–10in). Flowers divided into five lobes. Rounded leaves in a rosette at base of stem. Grassland, moors and gardens. July–September.

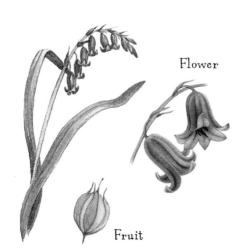

Flower

Fruit

Bluebell

30cm (12in). Also called wild hyacinth. Clusters of flowers. Shiny leaves. Grows in thick carpets in woods. April–May.

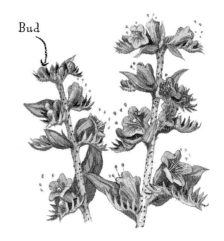

Bud

Viper's bugloss

30cm (12in). Pink buds become blue flowers. Long, narrow leaves on rough, bristly stems. Roadsides and sand dunes. June–September.

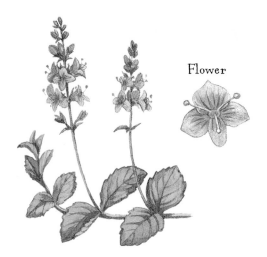

Flower

Heath speedwell

30cm (12in). Flowers grow in upright spikes. Hairy, oval leaves. Grows close to the ground in grassy places and woods. May–August.

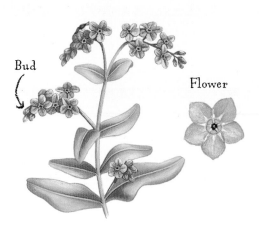

Bud

Flower

Forget-me-not

20cm (8in). Pink buds become tiny, blue flowers. Furry leaves. Open places, farmland and gardens. April–October.

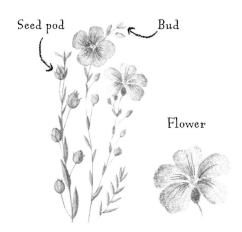

Seed pod   Bud

Flower

Blue flax

30–100cm (12–39in). Flowers have silky petals. Narrow, spear-shaped leaves. Meadows and roadsides. June–August.

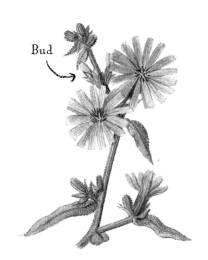

Bud

Chicory

30–120cm (12–47in). Flowers are usually blue or, very rarely, pink or white. Waste ground, roadsides and hedgerows. July–October.

Sea holly

20–60cm (8–24in). Flowers packed closely together in round flower heads. Spine-tipped leaves. Sandy and pebbly beaches. July–August.

Common milkwort

5–35cm (2–14in). Clusters of flowers that can be blue, pink, lilac or white. Grassy places and sand dunes. May–September.

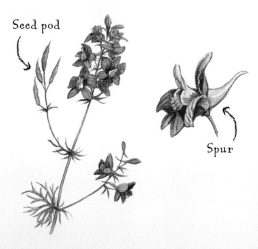

Cornflower

40cm (16in). Scaly leaf-like structures beneath cluster of flowers. Cornfields, waste ground and gardens. July–August.

Larkspur

50cm (20in). Spikes of purple, pink or white flowers. A spur sticks out behind each flower. Feathery leaves. Waste ground. June–July.

Pasque flower

10cm (4in). Purple or white bell-shaped flowers. Silky petals and stem. Deeply divided leaves. Gardens, rare in meadows. April–May.

Snake's head fritillary

10cm (4in). Rare in Europe. Can be pinkish-purple and checked, or white with faint pink or green veins. Damp meadows and woods. March–May.

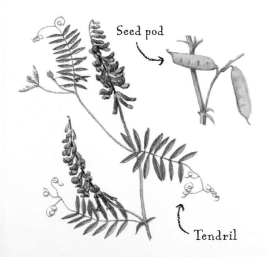

Seed pod

Tendril

Flower

Tufted vetch

50cm–200cm (20–79in). Climbing plant with curly, leaf-like tendrils. Hedges, roadsides and woods. June–September.

Foxglove

150cm (59in). Spotted, trumpet-shaped flowers that usually grow on only one side of the stem. Woods and grassy banks. June–September.

Flower

Flower

Cuckoo flower

15–50cm (6–20in). Flowers are pale lilac, sometimes white. Wet meadows, marshes and hedgerows. April–June.

Wild pansy

15cm (6in). Bright flowers that are often three-coloured. Oval leaves. Farmland, waste ground and gardens. April–October.

Fruit

Bloody crane's-bill

30cm (12in). Also known as blood-red geranium. Bright, pinkish-purple flowers. Hairy stem. Cliffs and meadows. June–August.

Common dog violet

10cm (4in). Creeping plant with rosettes of heart-shaped leaves and pointed sepals. Woods and hedges. March–June.

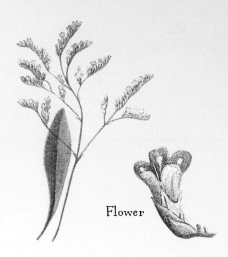

Flower

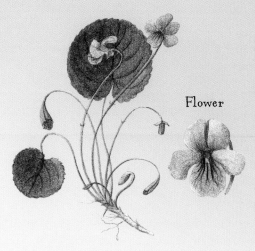

Flower

Sea lavender

20–50cm (8–20in). Purple flowers
with yellow anthers. Slender, wiry
stems. Salt marshes, often grows in
large clumps. July–September.

Marsh violet

5–50cm (2–20in). Lilac flowers
with dark purple veins. Heart-
shaped or kidney-shaped leaves.
Marshes. April–July.

Columbine

30–100cm (12–39in). Flowers are
usually purple or blue, but can be
pink or white. Wet meadows, open
woodland and hedgerows. May–July.

Early purple orchid

60cm (24in). Flowers usually purple,
but sometimes pink or white.
Purple-tinged stem. Dark spots on
leaves. Woods and hedges. April–July.

Seed pod

Common poppy

60cm (24in). Upright plant with stiff hairs on stem. Round seed pods grow in late summer. Cornfields and waste ground. June–August.

Sweet William

60cm (24in). Flat cluster of flowers. Pink or mauve petals with a spicy scent. Farmland, roadsides and mountains. May–June.

Flower

Unripe fruit

Scarlet pimpernel

15cm (6in). Creeping plant. Blue flowers sometimes found growing alongside the more usual red ones. Farmland. June–August.

Sorrel

20–100cm (8–40in). Also known as spinach dock. Clusters of tiny flowers. Grows in large patches in meadows. May–July.

Flower

Heather

20cm (8in). Also known as ling.
Tiny, pink or white flowers.
Overlapping leaves. Grows in
carpets on moors. July–September.

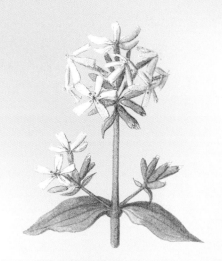

Soapwort

30–100cm (12–39in). Flowers are pale
pink, sometimes white. Pale leaves with
three veins. Waste ground, hedgerows
and roadsides. May–September.

Flower

Great willowherb

100–200cm (39–79in). Flowers usually
pink, occasionally white. Hairy leaves
and stems. By rivers and streams, and
in damp meadows. June–September.

Seed pod

Red campion

60cm (24in). Dark pink flowers.
Also comes in white and pale pink
varieties. Hairy leaves and stem.
Woods. May–June.

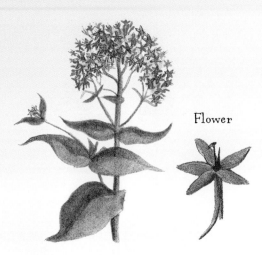

Flower

Ragged Robin

30–70cm (12–28in). Bright pink, raggedy petals. Also comes in white. Marshes and damp meadows. May–July.

Red valerian

30–80cm (12–32in). Flowers can be red, pink or white. Coastal rocks and cliffs, old walls, sandy places. May–September.

Seed pod

Flower

Herb Robert

40cm (16in). Flowers have a strong, unpleasant smell. Hairy leaves and stem that turn red in autumn. Woods and hedges. May–September.

Rest harrow

10–70cm (4–28in). Flowers can be pink or purple. Leaves covered with sticky hairs. Dry, grassy places and sand dunes. June–September.

Wood woundwort

50–120cm (20–47in). Toothed leaves that give off a strong, unpleasant smell. Woods, hedgerows and roadsides. July–September.

Policeman's helmet

100–200cm (39–79in). Flowers can be pink, purple or white. Leaves are edged with red teeth. By rivers and streams. July–October.

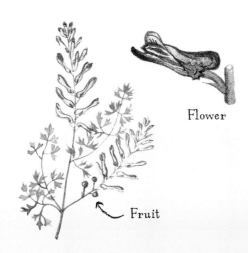

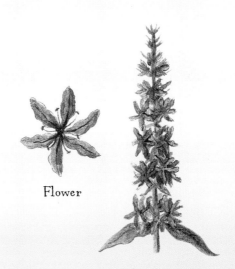

Fumitory

20–100cm (8–39in). Grey-green leaves. Small, round fruit. Waste ground, roadsides and hedgerows. March–November.

Purple loosestrife

50–180cm (20–71in). Hairy stem and leaves. Grows in clumps on marshes, and by streams and rivers. June–September.

Rose hip
(fruit)

Dog rose

3m (10ft). Sweet-scented, pink or white flowers. Thorny stems. Shiny, red, fruits develop in autumn. Hedges and woods. June–July.

Snowdrop

20cm (8in). Drooping flowers with honey-like scent. Slender stem and long, flat leaves. Comes in several varieties. Woods. January–March.

Bud

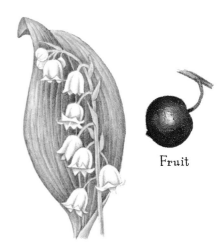

Fruit

Greater bindweed

3m (10ft). Climbing plant. Large, white flowers, sometimes with pale pink stripes. Hedges and riverbanks. July–September.

Lily-of-the-valley

20cm (8in). Sweet-smelling flowers. Two wide, shiny, leathery leaves. Bright orange-red berries in summer. Woods and gardens. May–June.

Fruit

Fruit

Goosegrass

60cm (24in). Climbing plant. Tiny, white flowers. Leaves, stem and fruit covered with hooked bristles. Hedges. June–September.

Blackberry

3m (10ft). Also known as bramble. Sharp prickles on stems and under leaves. Berries grow in autumn. Hedges and woods. June–September.

Flower

Wood anemone

15cm (6in). Also called granny's nightcap. Petals are white with pink streaks on the outside. Grows in large patches in woods. March–June.

Yarrow

60cm (24in). Flat-topped clusters of white or pink flowers. Rough stem and feathery leaves. Hedges and meadows. June–August.

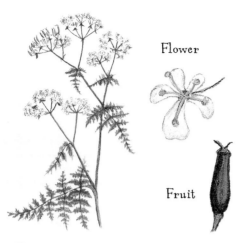

Flower

Fruit

Closed
flower
head

Cow parsley

100cm (40in). Also called Lady's lace.
Clusters of tiny flowers. Ribbed stem
and feathery leaves. Hedge banks,
roadsides and ditches. May–June.

Oxeye daisy

60cm (24in). Flowers close at night.
Large leaves at base of stem, smaller
leaves further up. Gardens and
waste ground. June–August.

Long veins
on leaf

Ramsons

10–25cm (4–10in). Also known as
wild garlic. Flowers have strong,
garlicky smell. Long, shiny leaves.
Damp, shady woods. April–June.

Scented mayweed

60cm (24in). A fast-growing plant
with feathery leaves and an apple-
like scent. Farmland and waste
ground. June–July.

Closed
flower
head

Daisy

10cm (4in). Rosette of leaves at base of stem. Flowers close at night and in bad weather. Most grassy places. January–October.

White dead-nettle

60cm (24in). White or greenish-white lipped flowers. Hairy leaves that don't sting. Hedges and waste ground. March–November.

Four-leaf
clover

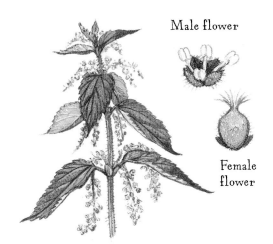

Male flower

Female
flower

White clover

10–25cm (4–10in). Dense flower heads that are usually white or pale pink. Leaves have a white band. Parks, gardens and meadows. April–August.

Stinging nettle

100cm (40in). Leaves and stem covered with stinging hairs. Damp, shady spots, and woods by streams and rivers. June–August.

Flower

Lady's bedstraw

10–80cm (4–32in). Honey-scented flowers. Shiny leaves, hairy underneath. Dry, grassy places and sand dunes. May–September.

Creeping buttercup

10–50cm (4–20in). Shiny flowers. Long, trailing stems and hairy leaves. Grows close to the ground in grassy places. May–August.

Bud

Marsh marigold

10–45cm (4–18in). Shiny, saucer-shaped flowers. Toothed, heart-shaped leaves. Marshes and wet meadows. March–June.

Bud

Primrose

15cm (6in). Often first flower of spring. Soft, wrinkled leaves and hairy stems. Grows in patches in woods, hedges and fields. December–May.

St. John's wort

60cm (24in). Clusters of deep yellow flowers with many stamens. Black dots on anthers. Damp, grassy places. June–September.

Silverweed

10–30cm (4–12in). Leaves densely hairy underneath. Red runners. Grassland, roadsides and waste ground. May–September.

Bud

Sepals

Common rockrose

10–40cm (4–16in). Flowers can be yellow, cream or orange. Leaves are hairy underneath. Grassland and rocky ground. May–September.

Cowslip

15cm (6in). Golden-yellow flowers with long sepals. Rosette of long, crinkled leaves at base of stem. Meadows. April–May.

Fruit

Dandelion

15cm (6in). Square-tipped, yellow petals. Rosette of toothed leaves. Hairy, white seed head. Grassy areas and roadsides. March–June.

Monkey flower

10–50cm (8–20in). Bright yellow flowers with red spots. Square stems. Marshes, river banks and by streams. June–September.

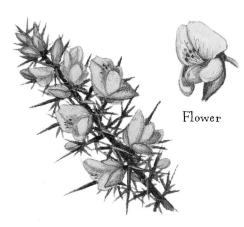

Flower

Ragwort

30–150cm (12–59in). Yellow flower heads. Fruits have "parachutes" of white hairs. Grassland and sand dunes. June-September.

Gorse

1–2m (40–80in). Also known as furze. Flowers smell like coconut and vanilla. Dark-green, spiny leaves. Moors and waste ground. March–June.

Seed pod

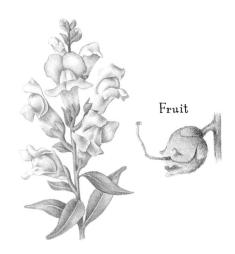

Fruit

Bird's-foot trefoil

10cm (4in). Also known as bacon and eggs. Creeping plant. Flowers are yellow with red streaks. Grassy banks. May–June.

Snapdragon

40cm (16in). Flowers come in lots of different colours, including purple, yellow and white. Gardens, rocks and old walls. June–September.

Flower

Kidney vetch

10–60cm (4–24in). Flowers can be yellow, orange or sometimes red. Thick, hairy sepals. Grassland, rocks and sand dunes. May–September.

Yellow rattle

10–50cm (4–20in). Yellow flowers with violet tips. Toothed leaves. Fruits are seed pods. Grassland and roadsides. May–July.

Glossary

Here are some words in the book you might not know. Any word in *italics* is defined elsewhere in the glossary.

anther The blobby tip of a *stamen*, where *pollen* is made.

bud An undeveloped flower or leaf.

bulb A thick, underground stem, covered in scaly leaves, which a plant uses to store food and produce new plants.

canopy The layer formed by the leaves and branches of trees in a wood.

climbing plant A plant that grows upwards using a wall, fence or other plant for support.

corm A short, swollen underground stem, which a plant uses to store food and produce new plants.

creeping plant A plant that grows along the ground.

field A large area of land, often used for growing crops and keeping animals.

fruit Part of a plant that holds its *seeds*.

heath An open area of windy, well-drained land.

leaflet A single part of a divided leaf that is made up of several separate sections.

lobed leaf A type of leaf or *leaflet*, partly divided into sections called lobes.

marsh An open, grassy area that is waterlogged for some or all of the year.

meadow A large area of land used for growing grasses to make hay.

moor An open area of land that is wet and windy.

nectar A sweet liquid made near the bases of petals to attract insects which will move *pollen* to another flower of the same type.

nutrients Chemicals that a plant needs for growth.

ovary The lower part of the *pistil* that contains *ovules*.

ovule A plant's "egg", which combines with a grain of *pollen* to make a *seed*.

petals Parts of a flower that surround the *pistil* and *stamens*. Petals are often brightly coloured.

pistil A female part of a flower. See also *stigma* and *ovary*.

pollen A powder made by a flower's male parts for transfer to the female parts to make *seeds*.

rhizome An underground stem that grows horizontally, and produces roots and leaves, which can develop into new plants.

root A part of a plant that anchors it into the ground, and absorbs water and *nutrients* from the soil.

rosette A circle of leaves growing from a single point.

runner A stem that grows along the ground, putting down roots that can grow into new plants.

salt marsh A low-lying coastal area, where the land is regularly flooded by sea water.

sand dune A large ridge of wind-blown sand.

seed A fertilized *ovule* that may grow into a new plant.

seedling A very young plant, that has grown from a *seed*.

seed pod A tough, dry *fruit*.

sepals Leaf-like parts that protect a flower while it is a *bud*.

spur A narrow, hollow cone at the base of a *petal* that sticks out behind a flower.

stamen The male part of a flower, where *pollen* is made. See also *anther*.

stigma The sticky tip of a *pistil*, to which *pollen* attaches.

tendril A slender leaf or stem, which twines around objects for support.

toothed leaf A leaf or *leaflet* with jagged edges.

weed Any plant growing where it is not wanted.

Index

Acknowledgements

Every effort has been made to trace the copyright holders of material in this book. If any rights have been omitted, the publishers offer to rectify this in any subsequent editions following notification. The publishers are grateful to the following organizations and individuals for their permission to reproduce material:

Cover © David Dixon/ardea.com; **p1** © age footstock/Superstock; **p2-3** © Bob Gibbons, Ardea London Ltd; **p4** © Robin Whalley/Alamy; **p6-7** © David Kjaer/naturepl.com; **p9** © Chris Gomersall/naturepl.com; **p18** © Rolf Kopfle, Ardea London Ltd; **p20** © South West Images Scotland/Alamy; **p22** © Dougal Waters/Photodisk Red/Getty Images; **p25** © Richard Taylor-Jones/Alamy; **p26** © Bob Gibbons/Science Photo Library; **p29** © Beata Moore/Alamy; **p31** © blickwinkel/Alamy; **p32** © ImageState/Alamy; **p35** © Tony Wharton/FLPA; **p36** © David Chapman/Alamy; **p39** © Ingram Publishing/Alamy; **p46-47** © Joe Mamer Photography/ Alamy; **p48-49** © Dietrich Rose/zefa/Corbis

Illustrators

Dave Ashby, Mike Atkinson, Graham Austin, Bob Bampton, John Barber, Amanda Barlow, David Baxter, Andrew Beckett, Joyce Bee, Stephen Bennett, Roland Berry, Isabel Bowring, Trevor Boyer, Wendy Bramall, Paul Brooks, Mark Burgess, Hilary Burn, Liz Butler, Terry Callcut, Lynn Chadwick, Frankie Coventry, Patrick Cox, Christine Darter, Sarah De Ath, Kevin Dean, Brin Edwards, Michelle Emblem, Denise Finney, Don Forrest, Sarah Fox-Davies, John Francis, Nigel Frey, Sheila Galbraith, William Giles, Victoria Gooman, Victoria Gordon, Teri Gower, Laura Hammonds, Nick Harris, Tim Hayward, Bob Hersey, Chris Howell-Jones, Christine Howes, David Hurrell, Ian Jackson, Roger Kent, Aziz Khan, Colin King, Deborah King, Jonathan Langley, Richard Lewington, Ken Lily, Mick Loates, Alan Male, Alan Marks, Andy Martin, Josephine Martin, Rodney Matthews, Uwe Mayer, Rob McCaig, Malcolm McGregor, Doreen McGuinness, Dee McLean, Richard Millington, Annabel Milne, Dee Morgan, Robert Morton, Patricia Mynott, David Nash, Barbara Nicholson, Richard Orr, David Palmer, Charles Pearson, Julie Piper, Gillian Platt, Maurice Pledger, Cynthia Pow, Mike Pringle, David Quinn, Charles Raymond, Barry Raynor, Phillip Richardson, Jim Robbins, Peter Scott, John Shackell, Chris Shields, Maggie Silver, Gwen Simpson, Annabel Spenceley, Peter Stebbing, Ralph Stobart, George Thompson, Joan Thompson, Joyce Tuhill, Sally Volke, Peter Warner, David Watson, Phil Weare, Adrian Williams, Roy Wiltshire, James Woods, David Wright, John Yates.

Cover design: Helen Wood
Additional designs: Joanne Kirkby and Reuben Barrance
Additional editorial contributions: Hazel Maskell and Kate Davies
Digital manipulation: Keith Furnival
Series editor: Jane Chisholm